Years ago, when we first conceived of writing something together, our plan was to make it a book for children. **Sisters First: Stories from Our Wild and Wonderful Life** *eventually became a memoir for adults, but we never stopped wanting to create something for young readers too.*

* **Sisters First** *is a love story to each other. Being born a twin was the luckiest thing that ever happened to us. We each had a constant companion, a playmate, and a friend, and our lives expanded as we were able to see the world through someone else's eyes. Having a sister made us braver than we ever thought we could be, whether we were sharing a bedroom in the White House or living thousands of miles apart.*

* As we've grown older, our definition of "sisters" has expanded to friends and colleagues—women who lift us up and help us believe that we are enough.* **Sisters First** *is a love story to them too, as well as to the next generation of girls. We feel so much happiness watching the magic of sisterhood flourish in our new loves, Mila and Poppy; we even used some of the things they've said and imagined in this book's text.*

* It is our wish for all women and girls—whether blood sisters or dear friends—that the power of sisterhood fills their lives with confidence and joy.*

For Mila and Poppy, who will be
sisters first forever and always
—JBH & BPB

For my sister, Jasmin
—RK

ABOUT THIS BOOK

The illustrations for this book were created using hand-painted textures and digital watercolor and pencil brushes in Photoshop. This book was edited by Deirdre Jones and designed by David Caplan and Kelly Brennan. The production was supervised by Ruiko Tokunaga, and the production editor was Jen Graham. The text was set in Georgia, and the display type is Gioviale.

Sisters First

JENNA BUSH HAGER &
BARBARA PIERCE BUSH
ILLUSTRATED BY RAMONA KAULITZKI

Little, Brown and Company

New York • Boston

Before there was you, there was only me,
and life was becoming a little lonely.

There were friends to laugh with and dogs to chase,
but I still said a prayer as I pictured your face:

Please make her kind, with an enormous heart,
clever too, and very smart.

With soft hands to hold and warm arms to hug,
and gentle eyes that show deep love.

My wishing paid off;
it was written in the stars:
A new baby sister would
soon be ours.

She'd be here in months,
so I had to prepare,
making flower crowns and forts
that one day we'd share.

And then—ta-da!—you finally arrived.
This little girl, this *one is mine*—
and she'll stay with me till the end of time.

Your eyes were so tiny, your fingers curled.
I shouted, "My sissy will rule the world!"

But you were different, much smaller than me;
you didn't play tag or sing...we didn't always agree.

You cried and you ate, but not much more.
(My new baby sister was a bit of a snore.)

Tears leaked from my eyes, and I wanted to pout...
until I thought of my prayer, and what it was about.

Please make her kind, with an enormous heart,
clever too, and very smart.

With soft hands to hold and warm arms to hug,
and gentle eyes that show deep love.

If kindness was what I was asking of you,
I needed to be kind and patient too.

And with time...we found a rhythm, your hand locked in mine.
We sang duets and danced in rain and sunshine.

Sisters are partners (mainly in crime).
We play tricks on our parents
and sneak treats at bedtime.

We're kitchen magicians, making crazy concoctions.
Pickles dipped in sprinkles is our favorite option!

And because of you, my imagination expands:
now superhero sisters and the toys we command.

With you next to me, we can even be...
cat pirates sailing across the rough sea!

We're splashy mermaids waving at freighters,
and when we tire, we ride our pet alligators.

As friendly coyotes, we howl at the moon
and stomp in a circle, singing a tune.

We ride in balloons to visit the clouds,
then tap-dance for the stars, taking our bows.

In our high heels, we become president and VP;
we give speeches and sing of the "land of the free."

With you by my side, I'm braver than before.
You love me for me and hold my hand when unsure.

Monsters are still scary, and I still fall down, but your
sweet, loving presence turns my bad days around.

Dear sissy, as you grow older, you won't always smile—
it's bound to happen every once in a while.

But I will be near to sing you a song, rub your back,
make you laugh, and cheer you along.

And the prayer of your birth we still say to this day,
for ourselves and for all sisters making their way:

Please make us kind, with enormous hearts,
clever too, and very smart.

With soft hands to hold and warm arms to hug,
and gentle eyes that show deep love.

Accepting and patient, yet strong in our views,
hopeful and joyful in all that we do.

And through many days, the best and the worst,
help us remember we are sisters first.